D1520248

# LIKE A FIELD RIDDLED BY ANTS

*fictions of*

Myra Sklarew

# LIKE A FIELD RIDDLED BY ANTS

Lost Roads  ∅  Number 32  ∅  1987

Library of Congress Cataloging in Publication Data
Sklarew, Myra   Like A Field Riddled by Ants
    (Lost roads series; no.32)
    I.   Title.
PS3569.K57A83        1987        813'.54        87-16961
ISBN 0-918786-36-3

Published by Lost Roads Publishers
P. O. Box 5848 Weybosset Hill Sta.
Providence, Rhode Island   02903
First Printing by McNaughton & Gunn


Cover Painting "Uneven Pair" by Douglas Canfield
Book Design by Forrest Gander and C. D. Wright


This project is supported by a grant from the National Endow-
ment for the Arts in Washington, D.C., a federal agency.

ALSO FROM LOST ROADS

Poetry

Ralph Adamo,   *Sadness at the Private University;*
*The End of the World*
Irv Broughton,   *The Blessing of the Fleet*
Justin Caldwell,   *The Sleeping Porch*
Mark Craver,   *The Problem of Grace*
quinton Duval,   *Dinner Music*
Honor Johnson,   *Small As a Resurrection*
Frances Mayes,   *Hours*
John McKernan,   *Walking Along the Missouri River*
John S. Morris,   *Bean Street*
Stan Rice,   *Body of Work*
Frank Stanford,   *The Singing Knives; You;*
*The Battlefield Where the Moon Says I Love You*
Arthur Sze,   *River, River*
Carolyn Beard Whitlow,   *Wild Meat*

Fiction

Alison Bundy,   *A Bad Business*
Mary Caponegro,   *Tales from the Next Village*
Steve Stern,   *Isaac and the Undertaker's Daughter*

In Translation

René Char,   *No Siege Is Absolute*  versions by Franz Wright
Philippe Soupault,   *I'm Lying*  translated by Paulette Schmidt

Art

Zuleyka Benitez,   *Trouble in Paradise*

Travel

Barbara and Sandra Heller,   *New Orleans My Darling*

Poetry by Myra Sklarew

From the Backyard of the Diaspora     *Dryad Press,*
*1981*
In the Basket of the Blind     *Cherry Valley Editions,*
*1975*
Blessed Art Thou No One     *Chowder Chapbooks,*
*1981*
The Science of Goodbyes     *University of Georgia,*
*1982, 1983*
Travels of the Itinerant Freda Aharon     *Watermark*
*Press, 1985*
Altamira     *Washington Writers Publishing House, 1987*

*for my washington hearts*

"In the Afterlife which is a Library" received the PEN Syndicated Fiction Award in 1983; "Certainty" was published in the *Webster Review*; "Valentine's Day" was published in PEN Stories by the Available Press (Ballantine Books) in 1985; "Speech Warts" was published in *The Science of Goodbyes* by the University of Georgia Press, 1982, 1983; "Albino" and "The Messenger" were reprinted in *Lilith*. "Getting There" received the PEN Syndicated Fiction Award for 1986 and "Interruption" won the PEN Syndicated Fiction Award for 1987. "At the Door to that Room," "There," "Looking at Men," "Where We Are Led," and "Speech Warts" appeared in a different form in *Altamira*, WWPH, 1987.

With special thanks to Michael S. Harper and to Robert Coover.

# CONTENTS

Speech Warts /13/

The Interruption /15/

At The Door To That Room /23/

Acquisitions /26/

Certainty /35/

Looking At Men /39/

The Guardians Of The First Estate /42/

In The Afterlife Which Is A Library /48/

Hermeneutics /51/

Niels Bohr And The Elephant /52/

The Messenger /56/

Albino /61/

Where We Are Led /65/

Whose Hands Are These /67/

Saturday Afternoon At The Movies /72/

A Little Sex Goes A Long Way /73/

Getting There /78/

There /85/

Valentine's Day /87/

Mushroom /91/

# Speech Warts

Fetch me a red flower from that meadow, says Ludwig. I look at him. Which shade of red? What species of flower? And on what green stalk? He is silent. How shall I get there without losing the flower on the way to the meadow, the one he has imagined, the idea of the flower which he has presented to me. I take a sheet from my left pocket which contains the shapes of all English and American flowers. I take a glass prism from my right pocket. Now I march up to the nearest meadow and compare real flowers with my chart of flower shapes. I pass a ray of sunlight through my prism and produce a color band which I compare with the colors of the flowers. But the flowers in the meadow are in foreign languages: Sprechenvorts! Gehimmel-hymenoptera! they shout at me. Louloudia, they continue to berate me, this time in Greek, mocking my shape grilles, my color bands. What next? I ask him. Fetch me the meadow, he says. Be quick about it. I come back, my arms full. I can barely walk under the weight of sumac, wild barley, their names heavy in Russian, Serbo-Croatian, various Indo-European tongues. My face is a sheath of red flowers. Not the one I had imagined, he tells me. Not that one, he repeats. Nowhere to be found in the vast meadow you have brought me, he whispers sadly. I set down the meadow before him. I take a sheet of paper from my hip pocket. I write on it: A RED FLOWER FROM THAT MEADOW, and I attach it to a stick which I set upright, waving, in the center of the meadow. That one, Ludwig whispers gratefully. That is the one.

# The Interruption

*Some people can do many things at a time without worrying, but as soon as I interrupt my work my heart feels sad, like a bookcase empty of books or a field riddled by ants.*

S. Y. Agnon

At first, the interruptions were of no consequence. Like the locket of air contained in a keyhole. Later, they widened, like a doorway. Gradually the number of interruptions increased like the number of days which pass in a year until I felt in myself a constant yearning which I could not name. As I moved through the long days, a certain tune accompanied me—the kind sung by the women suspended in the wire cages of the great mental institutions of long-gone days, desperate cries for help disguised in elaborate rhymes. The women—their pale faces pressed between the bars, their bony knuckles pushed up from beneath the skin like miniature heads of the cabbalists pushing up from beneath their prayer shawls. Whatever I did the song commanded me, It grew ragged, insistent.

For what I did not claim of this world and shape in my hands—like the potter making from the dust his infinite shapes, like the Golem who rises from a few grains—I could not know. Like a swimmer who does not swim, my legs and arms forgot how to live in the water. They became suitable for the land alone. And I dreamed of water every night.

∅

So I set about guarding my life. I built a fence around it. To the north I constructed a boundary of ice boulders. To the east, a wall of leaves. To the west, light. And to the south, water. Only the earth was allowed within. And what few birds could fly above the barriers I made for myself. And for many years I went on this way.

∅

Gradually I began to listen to others. There came one day a man to my door who insisted on his claim for my attention. Perhaps, he urged, my message is of more consequence than the words you commit yourself to with such fervor. So from then on I listened anxiously for the stranger. Who, I wondered, could fall in to my realm from the world? Oh, how I longed for any disturbance: the slightest step in the hall, a rap on the window, a branch scratching aimlessly along the roof.

∅

Why then should anticipation have caused me such grief? I dared not lift my pen to write a word, so poised was I for the possibility, for what might enter the silence. The ink dried in the inkwell. The tip of the pen hardened. The words fell back into that place where words begin to form. The dreams left my house and took up residence elsewhere.

Ø

Why do you regard what could happen with such morbid anxiety? Franz wants to know. When I, he goes on, hear the sounds of footsteps approaching my room, I listen eagerly to distinguish this pair of feet from all others. To flee from the miraculous, to avoid the unexpected—that is cowardice. In that one coming toward you is contained the perfect question, laying open every secret like a finger pointing the way. You may travel there when you discover whose footprints have walked through the sifted ash and who has rubbed against you wearing out your clothes and who surrounds you like a ridge around a field. What, you must say, of the world will this stranger offer me. What, that I wouldn't have access to myself.

Ø

Or my way, Johann urges me. Do you hear those donkeys braying in the middle of the tune I've just made up? They are the church fathers demanding that I make them a work of art. I have made them their music, a work we will never forget, though they do not know enough to realize how they have grown donkey's ears and tails. It is my own joke, he tells me.

Ø

Once, the guns started—rockets firing from the north. We who have fought over how the land should be used—whether for shelters or for growing carrots, potatoes, onions—fled not to the garden which had used up most of the space above ground, but to the shelter which we had dug below ground. Down the concrete stairs we fled while the rockets sang over-head, down to the bunkers. I carried a child in one arm, a manuscript in the other. I was like the garden, only making a small concession to the rockets.

∅

Even there, between the metal cots, in the dank stony air, I went on dreaming. The stories flew from my pen. No further interruptions; for were we not all gathered together, as under the tabernacle of fruits and vegetables in the ritual of the fall harvest. Only here we had no access to the star of morning, the first star of evening. We went on praying as though we could visualize the cosmos, though time was abolished in this place.

∅

Now, I thought, nothing can disturb me. Not war, not the ominous footsteps. For there were no halls, no hidden spaces. Only a large room filled with bunks. But death visited us. And who cannot stop his scrib-bling for death.

The one death chose was not ready, And when death entered his body, he protested mildly at first and then with all his might until his wife and sons had to hold him down so he could succumb to the cold that climbed through the latticework of his body. Now who could say that this was not an interruption. Who could find fault with the stopping of work. That for a few days nothing more should be said. Or done.

And when they committed him to the earth, time stopped again. The hands of the clock went around once, and once again. And then they rested. As on the sabbath, they did no more work. Only the laborers came to turn up the earth like sheets in a bed and make a place for him, among the others. Just as the men from the burial society had come the day before and taken his body and washed it and said their prayers over him.

When we came up from below ground and returned to our houses, we were grateful again for the air, for the song of the rockets whizzing by overhead to have ceased. In its place, the night songs of the cicadas. For it was their season. Everywhere one could see the swollen mounds where they had fled the earth for their brief sojourn above ground and the cycle by which they are born again. How they dared to shed their outermost garment, all that stood between them and the jaws of some rodent, we cannot say. But proof of it lay in the crisp exoskeletons attached to a leaf, while they themselves were elsewhere, above us. Drying, their white bodies hardening and taking on color until they became fully adult, they made ready to enter the choir above us, the buzz of throaty chanting back and forth among the poplars and eucalyptus trees.

In the early morning I came upon a brother of the cicada, a bright green beetle with patches of irridescence and shading along its back in precisely the arrangement of color in the yew bushes. The beetle lay helplessly on its back wheeling its legs in the air. I brought a twig near for it to grasp and twirled it around so the creature was upright once more and set it upon the yew bush noticing as I did how its antennae ended in a three-pronged structure which could expand and contract at will. I thought no more about the green beetle, other than to acknowledge the small voice within which uttered a final "God's handiwork" as I parted from it and went back to work.

But later that night, long after midnight, I was returning to my house, nothing for company but a piece of a moon and a few clouds and that endless choir of cicadas, when I put the key into the lock and heard a sudden cry of distress. I looked down to see that in my approach I had injured a cicada. It lay on its back, its enormous wings under it like the palette used to carry the wounded. Its bright green body, the black shading, and under all of it a thin trail of mucus.

Oh those wings, lacework of veins like the threads of a girl's long hair when it flows in a river and, connecting it all, that substance like translucent glass stretched across its frame.

The creature cried out when it was struck. Cried out only once and lay still. Who has said that insects feel no pain? Here was proof then. And that small cry seared into me. I opened the door and went in. And did nothing more about it.

What does the Talmud say? Do not leave your brother on the steps to suffer his pain alone. But bring him into your house that he may take nourishment with you and refresh himself.

In my sleep that night I who had long ago given up dreaming of cigarettes was smoking a cigarette while around me families of cidadas were emerging from the dust and rising into the rafters, singing.

So there are those things which rise up from the earth and approach us. And that which falls to us from above. There are the celestial cities which hover over our own cities; there are the underpinnings of the world which hold us aloft. We had once held that what came to us from below, from out of the earth, was good, the harvest in its season. And what fell upon us from above was good as well. For who has not longed to catch a glimpse of Ezekiel's wheel humming with angels and figures from the other world. Or to see the Messiah being brought forth out of the land made of the fervent prayers of generations through Elijah's offices.

∅

But what came this day, what rose up from the earth and entered the heavens and came down to us was not that which we longed for, which we waited for during the times of our greatest suffering. For it was man-made. The first who beheld it were the herds of reindeer in the north. The particles fell upon them as they moved into their summer hunting grounds. But so imperceptibly they were unaware of it. And into the milk of the females. And into the cells of them all, so that the peoples of the north could no longer feed their young from the reindeer as they had for over three thousand years.

And in the warmer climates, high up in the mountains, the summer crops were being prepared and harvested and stored for the winter. The milk from the goats was drying in the sun; the cheese was ripening on the porches. The potatoes were being pulled from the earth. And the legumes were drying. The particles fell upon these things. And the small mouths on the undersides of leaves which drew to themselves moisture and certain gasses welcomed the new element whose particles crept into them. And in the light which flowed from the west the particles came, coloring the sky. Never was the sunset more beautiful than now. And in the blue glaciers, the particles drifted and entered as though all the doors of the houses had been left open.

Ø

And those who dwelled in this world went streaming out of their habitats: from their caves and their ice houses, from the trees and valleys, all who could crawl out of the sea, and those in the mountains, all went out over the earth in search of some place of safety.

For my part I have gone back into the house, my body bearing its own share of the particles, enough for myself and my descendants. Even now the changes are being wrought in places too small to visualize. Even now the interruption continues and I yield to it as though it had something to offer me, some wisdom or message if only I could read it.

And we all of us coat the earth with our shapes like a field which bears the motion of ants—quick signals where only moments before they had been—the quivering instantaneous signals of their passage as they swarm over the field on their way to reconstruct what has been broken into, as they hurry on their way to fill out whatever form and shape the future has devised.

# At The Door To That Room

Say you were born in a chicken coop. The first thing you remember is looking out from your slot. The bantam cocks are crowing in the next bin. Say you were comforted by scaly yellow legs rising in a ring around you. That you flew off the perch with your feathers whirring like there were motors inside.

For a time you got separated from the others. High up in a room off a hall you spelled out your name on the ceiling and the morning sun came to fill in the letters with light.

Each road ends at the door to that room. Just as the light begins to withdraw from the ceiling and long before the first star comes centering itself in the dark window, hovering uncontrollably like the body's shudder.

Below, doors open. A man and a woman make promises they will abandon in the first light. A dog barks out in his dream. The red fox makes his rounds past the woodpile. The room sails down the green lawn toward the white fountain. On a table, notes inside thin folded papers whisper to each other.

In the schoolyard, a girl standing on her head watches a red stain spread across the bottom of her gymsuit. A boy throws a rock into a yellow jacket's nest and sets you down onto it. You run, bees coming off your head like a jet stream rushing east.

You knit a khaki scarf twenty feet long for your uncle in North Africa. This is during the war. He comes back alive, still stuttering, with perfume in narrow vials.

You have a radio so large you could walk into it. On a wall high up in a world you haven't come in, a boy takes off his clothes and lies down. Soldiers with machine guns patrol just beneath him. He isn't starving yet, his father hasn't been gassed. He trades his ration of bread for a book.

In the twisted wires of a fence, a bird hangs upside down by its feet. You hold a black beetle in the palm of your hand, its legs moving like a locomotive. For months you dream of shark, barracuda, dolphin. Your father comes home one night with a wooden barrel. He digs a hole among his tomato plants and sets the barrel into the earth. He fills it with water and fish. The water leaks out between the staves. The fish glue themselves against the bottom of the barrel.

In that country, a mother and father sit halfway up the stairs getting the news. The ashes of their dead sisters and brothers float up the staircase and fall onto their bodies. The Polish piano teacher calls out to the Mother of God every time you put your fingers on the keyboard. You hide on the floor of her closet holding her green satin shoes. On the way home your sister will try to lose you again.

Somewhere in the house a woman is crying. The mirrors are covered with black cloths. The lid of the piano is closed. You do not kiss the face of the grand-mother in the box that has two holes in the bottom so she can leak out. Nothing will be the same again. The father with the barrel and the fish has gone into the earth. On Main Street, Fortunato is still standing in his doorway waiting for the next fire. And Vinnie Gallo is sliding all the way down to the bottom of the scale on his alto sax.

# Acquisitions

Two days before the birth, a hundred Brown Shirts forced the Liutpold Cinema to bring to an abrupt end its showing of the film, *The Girl from Vienna*. The Nazis had carefully prepared the demonstration, rising from their seats at the first love scene, crying out: "Shame! Scandal! Loyal Germans must leave!" This continued until the management was forced to abandon the showing.

In the evening edition of the newspaper, December 17, 1934, it was announced that 318 of Napoleon's letters had been discovered. During the horrors of the retreat when he lost 90,000 men, he preserved great nonchalance, giving little notice to the disaster of his men, worrying only that the Russians must be intercepting some of his letters to Marie Louise. "It is very cold—I am in perfect health—be gay and happy—never doubt my love," he wrote. Or "Do not be too familiar with the King of Spain, keep him at a distance . . . do not let him advise you upon your bearing or way of living, you know better than he."

There were other matters which claimed the reader's attention that evening: a man-eating fish; the problem of acceptable bathing suits in Sydney, Australia.

∅

*When alone, the infant is able to become unintegrated, to flounder, to be in a state in which there is no orientation, to be able to exist for a time without being either a reactor to an external impingement or an active person with a direction of interest or movement. The stage is set. In the course of time there arrives a sensation or an impulse. It is only under these conditions that the infant can have an experience that feels real.*

On the anniversary of the evening of her birth Ana dreamed that a school of fish had assembled above her and swam freely until she rose into their midst, disturbing them. Someone was holding up three straws, urging her to choose one. She took all three. A woman buried in winter called to her saying: My sister, saying Bride-cake and Long Life. A man newly buried refused to settle into his bones. He whispered: Tie the knot, tie the knot. Ana tried to call to him: Father, father . . . but there were clods of earth caught in her throat.

The dark-haired women held her upright. She was in a chariot that had driven all night through an ancient street, her feet out in front of her. It halted suddenly before a grillwork of bright blood.

When Ewald asked her what she had been dreaming about that had caused her to draw in her breath so sharply, she didn't answer him. For the first time, she knew beyond any doubt that hers had been a breech birth.

∅

—Why are your hands so cold? Ewald wants to know.

—It's the history, Ana tells him as he blows on her fingers with his warm breath at the same time that he prevents her from wrapping herself around his body. The history blowing through these rooms, Ana continues. The old story of exile and assassination.

—And your toes? What about these icy toes? Ewald asks her, cradling her feet in his own.

—Jewish extremity, she answers laughing. Cold hands and cold feet. All that long history stretching back before Christ and the Magi. Or...going forth into who knows what new calamity.

—The history, Ana says again teasing him, warming to this dialectic. The way the history goes from one desert to another. or stalls——she says, walking her fingers along his thigh, letting them come to rest between his legs. In some cozy doctrine . . . like the yellow-backed antelope bedded down in straw, the afternoon sun encircling her.

$\varnothing$

*Every night human beings lay aside the wrappings in which they have enveloped their skin, as well as anything which they may use as a supplement to their bodily organs, for instance, their spectacles, their false hair, and teeth. When they go to sleep they carry out an entirely analogous undressing of their minds and lay aside most of their psychical acquisitions. Thus on both counts they approach remarkably close to the situation in which they began life. The psychical state of a sleeping person is characteristized by an almost complete withdrawal from the surrounding world and a cessation of all interest in it.*

—At night we suffer, Ana told him. A gang of teenagers with knives threatens me. I plead with them: Please don't! I believe that if I look at them closely, look into their faces, and they are required to look into mine, they will not be able to kill me. In the end they back off. I am relieved and take this as a sign that I will not be given the death sentence when the test is done in the hospital on Wednesday.

—So, Ewald turns to her, fully awake, you have never freed yourself from them. They still surround you: the child you were, always sick. The mother at the bottom of the stairs who threatens to desert you. The doctor with his warm penis in the child's hand. The father coming up the stairs at night.

—Yes, I have only to close my eyes. And the still figures begin to move again. The girl never stops her cycle of illness and recovery. For days she lies in that bed dreaming and making inventions, waiting for the darkness to swell up until her window is filled with it. Signals for her father to come home. At night she is afraid of fire. Fire will burn down the house. Fire will reach its long arms into her room and seek her out while she lies helplessly in her bed and take her down with it. At night she is afraid of her sister who stands by her bed pleading with her.

—Do you think, Ewald asks, they go on? And we go on? And we never come near one another? Do they die when we die? Or outlast us? That would be a joke, wouldn't it?

—That sickly one, living longer than me! Ana exclaimed. Imagine! Resting up for years so she could get to the finish line in excellent health and long after me. It seemed she was tending a more robust nature, that she would one day give rise to this other one. I should have been more careful.

Ø

Some time later the girl stepped out of her bed, left the house and entered a wood, passing her body along the high stems of hollyhock, sassafras, dry wheat and wild grasses. She slipped through the rows of wild growing things until she was invisible, taken into the fields where her body was free again and her spirit could fly above her. The fear of houses did not catch up with her here.

—The way she gave her body to others! Ana scoffed.

In the house at night the girl walked back and forth through the hallway, her jaw tight. All night death cupped her in its bare hands.

Ø

*It is said we live in the life zone—not so close to the star which is our sun as to vaporize water, not so distant as to cause water to exist in its frozen state.*

During the night the rain coming down passed through a frigid zone coating the trees and grass. Each twig was outlined in ice. Only the thick trunks of the oldest trees seemed to discourage ice from forming. The ground, still warm from the oddly beneficient December, had not frozen. But the water, before it came to earth, coated nearly everything.

The child motioned for Ana to come out of doors with her. She had something to show her. Ana put on boots and a coat, the child gave her a glove from her own left hand and they went out. The girl bent low under the branches of a young ash tree made rigid by its coating of ice particles. She entered the space between branches and trunk and leaned against the trunk, her body framed by the arc of branches weighed down with ice. The dark lines of twigs ran through the nodules of ice like nerve axons coated with myelin sheaths. Each outbranching of the tree, each curve was marked in light.

It was sound the girl was after. But Ana was dazzled by the light, by patterns that seemed deliberate as magnetic fields. The girl wanted to show her how each tree had a different pitch; each one its own sound. And if she touched the small trunk of a tree, the whole of the tree moved in synchrony. The same with a clump of yews.

Touch one stem and the entire four-foot length moved as one body, the hydrogen atoms bonded together. And each tree did have a distinct sound: a high-pitched creaking; a rustle; or a low, grinding wave of sound.

$\varnothing$

—So, Ana said, more to herself than to him as she moved toward the warmth of his sleeping body, we meet again in this life.

—What did you say? Ewald stirred himself beside her.

—Nothing. Nothing at all, Ana answered him, still caught in the light each twig and branch seemed to give off, looking now to see what had become of the child's glove, a glove for the left hand. It was nowhere to be found.

$\varnothing$

During the night a tree branch coated with ice split apart from its trunk and fell earthward, knocking hard against the asbestos roof and from there slid to the ground, its sound sufficient to stir the sleepers briefly until they could turn once, recompose themselves and continue dreaming. Ana was jarred enough by that event to retrieve a memory she had been searching for.

The girl had been hospitalized when she was nine. For eleven days. On the first night home as she sat at the dinner table with her sisters and mother and father, the sound of the knife and fork against the plate was so overwhelming she burst into tears.

Ø

The child slept in a narrow bed separated from the others by a glass partition and a curtain. On the table beside her was a bouquet of lilacs from her mother's garden.

The nurses came and painted her legs and the inside of her thighs with a bright red solution. She did not ask what they were preparing her for. They held her down. Doctors came with tubing and gloves, opening her legs and inserting a tube so that it went from her body to a container they placed under her bed. When they had all gone, she cried. Some time later she vomited. She believed she had filled the entire ward with her vomit, that forty beds floated in it.

She could hear the nurses complaining about having to clean her up. Later, much later at night a nun dressed in a white habit came to her and comforted her. In the morning a priest came through the ward and asked her to make communion.

Ø

*Leaves torn off like coins torn away from the eyes of the dead. No one saw where they went. Like the bones of a bird. Who has recorded the whereabouts of the missing doves? The leaves fell all day through the surface of the earth. The snow covered the seams where the leaves fell. Where they fell through the seamless world toward the great heated core.*

In the shallows, the soggy bark curved around trapped air and carried it downstream. Ana put her left foot down carefully. The way was muddy, full of ditches, malevolent. The sun, leaning backward against the horizon, poured a sudden gust of light into the uppermost crown of a tree. Near her body, darkness steeped. She moved quickly, measuring each step before she took the next. These were the last days. The hunger to store time, the strange long fall, these things enticed Ana. Though it was December, the willow held onto its leaves.

Like the warm currents of the gulf stream running in the northern waters, the icy air contained pockets of warmth. Ana noted these alternations but couldn't account for them. Inside her the child moved and turned. Even as she walked. As though to keep pace with her. She held her belly, her two hands over the ligaments of support. Overhead a white moon hung in the crevice formed by two sycamore trees, marking her place.

Ana closed her eyes. The pains took hold of her, causing her to draw breath cautiously. From the raised mound of her belly, a ring of pain started up like the waves of sound within the chamber of a stone bell, set loose by its metal tongue.

The sensation traveled down along her body. The child moved slowly away from its moorings within her. As Ana exhaled, the infant drew back for an instant. But the next circle of pain began and the child advanced another short distance.

Ø

A man had been following Ana that day, had watched as she entered the wood and set out after her, a man she had never seen before. As she leaned against the trunk of an ash tree, Ana looked up into the face of a stranger. Whatever it was he tried to say to her seemed to drift toward her from another place, another country. The words never reached her, only the fact of his presence, his hands on her. A man she could not recognize stood between her and the river, not moving at all.

Ø

On Tuesday, December 18, the newspaper cost 2 cents. It was going to rain or snow by evening. The day before it had gone down to 31 degrees. Twenty-eight people were shot in a Soviet round-up. Counting the executions in the Ukraine, the total dead was 103. Nine of the 37 who had been seized were still being held. Two men had drowned in the ice of the Delaware Bay. Ice floes had crushed their boots. Ice cutters and planes were helpless given the conditions. And the country was under the seige of an influenza epidemic. Over 4,000 were ill.

*Note: The italicized passage in Section 2 is by D.W. Winnicott; in Section 4, Sigmund Freud.*

# Certainty

I have begun to forget the meanings of words. Arieh writes to me from his settlement in the south to say that the khamsin has come early. In autumn. I look at the word for a long time: autumn. Does it come before summer? Before spring? Autumn: dusk? Autumn. I have lost it. Its certainty. The way it once had an irrevocable meaning, its definition contained in it like a nucleus. It wears that definition loosely now, like a hat which blows off in the slightest wind.

Arieh is coming home. It is better to write of a thing before it happens. Afterward one must deal with the facts. But before, one can imagine the whole event, add to it, embellish it. Before, the events stretch out in all their possible forms. She wakes up, goes to the door and finds him waiting there. Or, she is driving along the highway toward the north and his car passes hers. They stop to walk together along the wadi. They go a long way in silence. Or, she has just prepared the meal. And he comes in then. She takes his coat and sets him down to the table and serves him the cabbage and eggplant and tomatoes she has grown herself. The rosemary pointing up the flavor, the spokes of the herb like signals in the sauce.

Signals of warning? Autumn. The word has a buzz at the end that is felt at the back of the throat. The mouth opens on it and closes like the shell of a clam. Fall. In the northern hemisphere. In the southern hemisphere, that time from the March equinox to the June solstice. You see, each idea seemed perfectly clear once. Each word. Without conditions, without exceptions. Does the water in the tub drain out clockwise or counterclockwise? Which hemisphere is this, actually?

*In the zone of the doldrums the wind has almost stopped altogether. Horses harnassed to the equator can no longer pull the earth in its orbit, so affected are they by the intense heat.*

He writes that there are troop movements to the east. That they have had to rise early for two weeks to go on maneuvers. That the sudden activity has him worried. They cannot clear their heads during this time of the hot winds. They are irritable. He writes that there is a peculiar expectancy, the way a certain sound at a high frequency enters your consciousness and you suddenly become aware that your whole attention is fastened to it, that you have begun to wait for that moment when it will cease. Like pain.

It is not his custom to warn me of his arrivals. He likes a certain tension, a suspense about his comings and goings. I have grown to like that as well. And anyhow, it is a reminder that certainty is something we want, not a quality of this world, not of this life. For hasn't the old woman died without asking if we minded. Netka, how was it you didn't wait for me to come home, to come to your side that night? But just died, quietly, alone. And Chanah, after the weeks, a whole year at your side, you waited till I had gone home to my own bed to sleep before you relinquished this life. I arrived there that morning to find your face raised to the light, your mouth in a peaceful smile as though you had discovered something we weren't ever to know, as if you had gone over to a place we hadn't any business in. And anyway, what would I have done had I been there at that moment of leaving? Would it have been different?

Death. There's another one. Hearth, breath. Wreathe. Death. If I say it often enough, the word shakes off its meaning like the dust of the rug Semmel beats in his window, like the dress Yenne shakes, the slight shudder of her body inside. Only the thick feel of my tongue between my teeth when I come down on the final consonants, the muffling of sound like the cover of snow, like the blanket that covered Chanah's face that morning, when two strangers came to take her from the room.

*At Eilat there is a hot wind that comes from Africa. When you breathe it in, your nostrils burn. Your bare arms feel hot to the touch. Though you are out of doors, between desert and sea, breathing itself brings a sense of claustrophobia.*

The conversation begins as though it had never ended. As though he hadn't left. The odor of other places is on him. I try to decipher the geography of his passage. I make a map and I place him here, here. All the while he talks. I wonder if he has slept in the beds of other women. I wonder what they look like. He talks. I do not listen. Sometimes a word falls onto my plate. I pick it up idly on my fork and taste it. It is salty on the tip of my tongue. Another word. Sometimes bitter at the edges. At first I do not listen. It takes me a long while to gather up what was once between us, to take the words I have sent to others and call them in. Like a shepherd calling his flock at evening. I call them home so they can be his again.

I lay in the bed with my legs in the position of running. He on his side with his two arms in sleep out in front of him as though he were waiting to receive something. I imagine I am running down the stairs, turning off a light, washing clothes, cooking a meal. My thoughts race. Toward morning I turn to him, my breasts touch his back. I listen for the sound of his breathing which has become regular and deep. I try to imagine his dream. He turns toward me and I place my body between his outstretched arms.

# Looking At Men

Yesterday, a man asked me why I was traveling alone. If he were my husband, he would not permit me to go away. It says in the Koran, the woman is the comfort of the man's body.

∅

The men took turns picking leeches off each other's bodies. When the war ended, the smell of fresh soap make them vomit.

∅

A man and his son and a horse. The father says: Get up on the horse. As they journey they pass a jeering crowd. How can you let your old father walk while you ride? they ask the boy. The father climbs up behind his son and they continue on their journey. They pass a group of people working in a field. How can you both ride, wearing out your old horse? they ask. In the end the father and son carry the horse.

∅

I watch a man quicken as he crosses a mine field, as he climbs into a bunker and takes up his submachine gun.

Ø

Replacements have come for instruction. The sergeant picks up a smooth metal ring. Do you know, he looks into their boys' faces, what these can do?

Ø

Beneath me a man's head is the only marker as he walks the labyrinth of trenches; this one's never seen war. He feels the earth around his body, the closest he's come to his own grave.

Ø

At night a man smokes a cigarette when he cannot sleep. These are true stories of a personal nature.

Ø

From letters I know how a man wishes to be seen. From sleeping with him I know how a man is.

Ø

Under me a man holds perfectly still to see how long he can stay inside me without coming.

Ø

A man, partly blind, touches my back lightly with one finger to learn where he is in this world. I mistake it for love.

Lady, a man calls to me, beautiful lady, if only you knew what you wanted, I would show it to you.

Ø

# The Guardians Of The First Estate

Daughtergirl was set up for it. After years of sitting in the darkened examining room of an eye doctor's office. Her mother off in the distance. Her with her nearsighted eyes. Him with his penis set right out on the chair between them. He breathed hard. His hand searched for hers. The two hands hovered in the vicinity of his organ. And came down together gently on top of it.

The eye examinations were interminable. The small light of his ophthalmoscope shone for long periods onto the back of her retina, causing her rods and cones to discharge erratically. Her mother never guessed what was happening so near to her. And Daughtergirl at age six had never come this close to the private parts of a grown man. Why Dr. Kapoyr was willing to risk all for this brief probe was not something Daughtergirl knew enough to ask. But there in his elegant downtown, wood-panelled office it is very likely that half the girl-children of that city had direct contact with Dr. Kapoyr's organ.

The mysterious bit of life which lay beneath her small hand was soft beyond anything she had ever felt. And years later she could imagine its warmth and quickening, the tender surface as her hand rode up and down it, guided patiently by his own hand. She did not look down. Likely she would not have seen anything had she dared to. Between the darkness and her dim eyesight. But it was a time in her life, though she was curious enough, when she would have been too polite to look at what was occurring.

Her mother was given the chair of honor. Against the far wall. Her voice came crisply across the room from time to time as though from a distant yet fashionable part of London. "How are the child's eyes today, Dr. Kapoyr?" she would inquire. "Has there been any significant change since we were last here?"

And Dr. Kapoyr, fully into the business of enlarging his organ, as well as seeing to the dilation of the pupil of the eye, the better to have at the interior parts, would call back to her in a thin, abstracted voice, "Mrs. Mother-daughter, we will have our conference as soon as the examination is finished." This seemed to satisfy her. Doctors in those days were not to be trifled with.

Daughtergirl could feel the hairs curling out from his nostrils. The odor of tobacco and after-shave lotion. His breath on her face. Her eyelashes reflected back to her in the bare light his instrument gave off. And years later she remembered how the inside of his thigh felt through the white coat he wore. Through the finely tailored trousers. Though at the time she hardly knew which continent she was swirling through space on. She hardly knew the names of the various apparati she was so calmly manipulating.

She had been tripping, stumbling over things. Falling down. She had no idea that others saw more than she did. She couldn't see the blackboard at school and didn't realize for some time that she was supposed to be able to. Above all, Dr. Kapoyr restored the world to her by bringing it into proper focus.

∅

She was sitting in the front seat of her teacher's dark green Packard. This was years later, in a parking lot during a thunderstorm. Luc Choirloft (they had trimmed Lucretius down to a manageable size but tried unsuccessfully during all of 9th grade to find out what his mother called him) and her father were inside the high school attending a meeting on recent vandalism and delinquency. Her father had no idea at all that she was out there. Choirloft had set it up with her. That she would wait for him in his car.

Luc Choirloft was an interesting case. He was fond of American history. You could say it was one of his specialties. And pubescent girls. Medieval art. That was something he was big on. And pubescent girls. He brought his two main interests together on occasion in that perfect intersection so rare in life. He took the pubescent girls to the Cloisters where among the medieval statues and gothic ceilings he fondled first the statues and then the girls. Sometimes he did both at once, bringing into his employ both left and right arm.

There among the beatific faces of the young girls raised in prayer and offering to the heavenly Father, Lucretius Choirloft managed to feel up any number of girls in close range of the guards without ever incurring suspicion. Never once did an irate father or surprised guard catch him at his exploits. Often one or another of his subjects would think better of the enterprise and break away, hiding behind a cloistered figure for a brief moment. Choirloft knew the museum exquisitely well after all his years in it. He would come upon the poor girl crouched behind a madonna and lure her out again, starting up the whole hotly entertaining game once more. It was, in fact, this juxtaposition of becalmed madonna with pubescent girl that so set him off.

Daughtergirl and Choirloft played it closer and closer to the edge, always increasing the odds of discovery. They never knew if it was some perversity that was behind this or if the greater danger provided more excitement. Daughtergirl didn't know at the time just how much of the proceedings were her doing. Some, she decided in retrospect.

Choirloft would occasionally take her home to visit his wife and kids. Daughtergirl felt that she knew something about them all that they separately had no way of knowing. As she watched his wife diaper the baby. Or as she tiptoed into a child's room one night, with Choirloft holdlng her hand, to witness the peace of a small son sleeping.

Was it in the nature of men, she reasoned with her new-found logic, as with turtles and fish, to disseminate sufficient seed to guarantee the continuation of the species? Perhaps, she ventured, our own quite recent code of morality was simply an overlay that had nothing at all to do with survival. Suddenly the urge of men to inseminate with great frequency wherever it seemed feasible struck her as a profound virtue. Daughtergirl felt like standing up in the middle of the high school gymnasium and cheering for mankind and his abundant seed. She too longed to be the recipient of such life-giving force as her teacher had to offer. Which is why she was spread across the front seat of his Packard when he appeared, suddenly illuminated by a flash of lightning.

Choirloft had managed to slip out of the meeting just before it ended. In moments Daughtergirl's father would appear in the same parking lot, climb into the family's blue Plymouth shaped like a box turtle and drive off, never suspecting that his Gibson girl, his own sweet daughter was waiting, hot-blooded, in the front seat of Luc Choirloft's car, only a few feet away from where he was parked.

The question was: To which theory of teaching did our fated couple ascribe? Was it the "stuff an apple in the teacher's mouth and serve him up to the hungry student" variety? Or was it the "dump truck" method where the teacher loads up his blue dump truck, backs it up to the door of the classroom, unloads and drives off? Or a third: "infusion and exchange," where the student is responsible for at least part of what happens. And where the student, with the teacher's help, must undergo some basic change. Daughtergirl felt that she was about to make some essential contact with the third method.

Choirloft started up the Packard. The broken muffler let out a sputtering roar, dropping engine juice like a series of dashes across the asphalt surface. Daughtergirl pondered the condition of Choirloft's front seat. She wondered how many other girls had been there before her. She wondered what he said to them and how many more would take their turns long after she was gone from this place.

They drove out of the school parking lot and onto Main Street. It appeared to anyone who might think to look that Lucretius Choirloft was entirely alone that night. But when they pulled off the road and headed down the narrow stretch leading to the bay, Lucretius Choirloft's other half, his pubescence, leaned mightily against him, all the while his hand travelled as though on its own. It wound around her shoulder and down her arm, touching the fingers of her right hand. Slowly, slowly, it made its way along her plaid wool skirt until it came to the edge of the hem where it began its ascent. Those fingers moved deftly up under her slip, finding places even she hadn't known she had. "You're wet there," he told her admiringly. She couldn't tell if he was pleased with his prowess in causing that to happen or if he was imagining how pleasant it would be to place his organ inside that wetness. These were matters she hadn't read about or even discussed. He continued to work those fingers of his right hand until she was feverish.

Years later she thought of him. Of that moment in the old Packard with him. Of her own sexuality proclaimed and admired. And she thought of Dr. Kapoyr staring with sublime concentration through the dilated opening of her pupil into the great velvety darkness which lay just beyond his reach, while far below he fumbled for a small hand in order to begin a ritual he had generously participated in many times before.

# In The Afterlife Which Is A Library

In the afterlife which is a library I am in the stacks when one of my 413 sins walks up to me: Why didn't you answer my letter? it asks. What is your name? I say, looking at it curiously. We have paused near the Rashi commentaries. We obviously are both after the same thing.

I think to myself, I knew it wasn't good when my analyst told me to forget about guilt. But what, I had argued with him, should I do about the 613 good deeds I hadn't yet performed. He leaned back in his Viennese chair among the figurines he was always collecting. Sometimes I couldn't see his face for all the wood and soapstone, all the little fertility figures, the male house idols, the nubile girls. I couldn't think sometimes, it was so distracting.

He leaned back. All this talk, all my money and nothing comes to take away this terrible ache. If I could fill up the empty places with words, I would. But it doesn't work. I don't mention this to him though. I don't think he would understand. It's the same with hunger: it's hard to fill up on prepositions and adverbs.

So there he is, leaning back in his chair. I can see the whites of his legs where his socks don't quite meet the bottom of his trousers. I am distracted again. Meanwhile I am talking about Charles Darwin and his beloved barnacles, about the return of the Monarch butterfly to West Virginia. And he is asking me what I think the conflict is really about. And I am imagining I am in the back seat of a car with a boy who is seventeen and I am seventeen.

He is leaning back in his chair when your face comes around the corner again. He clears his throat waiting for me to speak and I feel guilty. All that money going by like minutes and nothing said. Still the silence. He leans back waiting. I try to open my mouth but each time I do, I find your face pressed against mine. He gives up waiting and starts to talk. What thoughts do you have about this silence? he ventures. Suddenly I am sitting on the front stoop in full moonlight with you. I am breathing in the cool spring air.

Meanwhile, back in the stacks I meet up with this fellow. I knew, I just knew it would be like this. They would all be waiting for me, waiting their turns. And he is there holding out all the letters he ever wrote to me demanding to know why I stopped writing to him. What could I say? What would you have said?

Another of my sins comes along: I sent you my man- uscript, my life's work and you never wrote to me. You never even read it. In a black bound journal which he is waving around in my face, I can see the blood stains, the salty residue of tears, the concentric circles like tree rings of spilled coffee, his lifework poured out. And I have ignored him, have been unresponsive. But the worst, the absolute worst is the young girl who stands shyly and accusingly in the corner. It was my birthday, she whispers to me, my sixteenth birthday and I wrote to you and I sent you my poems and you never answered my letter. You never sent me a critique of my thirty-seven poems. What could I say? What would you have said? I pressed in among the books hoping I could avoid the eyes of the rest of them. Suddenly someone came running down the aisle: You let the policy lapse, he was shouting at me. You didn't make the payments.

I crouch down beside Rabbi Nahman of Bratzlav. I lean down next to Rabbi Akiba, the gentle martyr who is still wrapped in the parchment scrolls of the Torah. It is true they are singed by the fire the Romans put to him years ago, but the letters are all intact. What do you have to say, Master? I whisper to Akiba, What can you advise me? I say urgently. But his reply is a terrible silence. I press in against Moses and Abraham. But I am not hidden from sight.

# Hermeneutics

As you approach the table you must ask yourself about the question which is the egg, the egg seated before you in its small porcelain cup. Is the egg feminine or masculine? Is a soft-boiled egg a noun? A name? A woman? This question will not be answered until much later. Let us call this a Delay. Does this egg contain additional connotative signals? Yes? You say it makes you think of Humpty Dumpty? Let us refer to that as the Past. We do not care for the Past. It is open to interpretation. Soon the waiter will come to remove the egg. Which is no problem since the egg is our invention after all. Since this hunger which you feel is also an invention. At the conclusion of this meal all the enigmas will be disclosed. Each part of the broken shell pieced together again. The vast hermeneutic egg sealed in its tomb. Put down your fork, this cup. Put away your hunger for the meal. It is not sufficient simply to eat. You will get filled up. Which has something to do with survival. Which, in the long run, is unimportant.

# Niels Bohr And The Elephant

It wasn't until I looked up, really looked up, that I saw the snow. Coming down over what had fallen three days before. And in the far corner of the garden something like a dark wing fluttered periodically.

A bird caught in a drift? Or Niels Bohr's small leather notebook in which he was always noting down significant items as he roamed out of doors. For instance: *In the second downward plunge of minuteness, from a scale of $10^{-8}$ to one of $10^{-13}$ centimeters, a contrast does not exist.*

In any case, if it was a bird, it couldn't survive for long. I watched carefully but did not make a move to help. Just as, the night before, standing at the door of the bar, I did not move while Albert E. went up behind Petronius' chair, whispered something in his ear and then flattened him.

Petronius—they called him Rocky—had his hand on me, for no reason I could figure. Something resolute

and dangerous in his face. He wasn't going to let go
of this. Funny thing the way the other six of them,
his buddies, never tried to warn him or slow him
down. He butt into our conversation. Why were we
so serious, he wanted to know. Didn't we ever have
any fun? he kept on. Wedging himself back in every
few minutes. Or holding up a candle, inviting me to
observe the landslide taking place inside the green
dotted glass. I never could resist looking at something
I hadn't seen before.

As I stared at the white molten wax, I felt his hand
on my waist again, felt his fingers slide down along
my hip and stay put. I had to remind myself that I
had never laid eyes on him before, that what he was
doing was provocative.

"Listen Rocky ..." Albert E's voice came from far
away. I listened for the way he addressed Rocky, the
sound of his voice. A challenge to Rocky's manhood.
The rule of this game. The other one would be obliged
to pick it up. To return the challenge.

*Return the challenge, said Niels Bohr. That's like throwing
an elephant in slow motion through the air. I think I'll
compose a hunting story. This elephant has come to a wat-
ering spot on a river when he encounters a large poster. In
one short sentence the anti-particle principle is explained.
Reading it, the elephant is enchanted, the hunters hiding
in the bush slip out, tie his legs securely with heavy ropes
and ship him to the Hagenbeck Zoo in Hamburg.*

The hand, the same hand that a moment ago had
rested securely on my thigh, was rising threateningly
upward toward the table. It was making the finger,
friends. Yes, the finger. Albert E. caught it and came

quickly to the boil. This was, after all, a first-order challenge. One any man would rise to.

"Howja like to be my roommate, Baby?" Petronius is working both fronts at once this time. "You've got the right image."

"Which image is that?" I say.

"Well," he begins thoughtfully, "not the second wife image, not the first wife image, not the girlfriend image. Something else," he says. The anti-image, I think to myself. Like anti-particles.

*Anti-particles, hums Niels Bohr, picking up on it right away. That's a good one. The electron jumps into the bed of the proton and the hydrogen atom is annihilated instantaneously in a burst of high-frequency radiation. A new principle, he says, his eye gleaming, according to which any theory suggested by a theoretican would become immediately applicable to his body. Thus you would be turned into gamma-rays before you could tell anybody about your idea.*

Albert E. is a big guy. The story is that big men have to guard against the full use of their strength because they could kill their opponent without intending to. At least that's what Albert E. told me. I look at his large body which is about to be belted across the table by his smaller opponent and wonder just where the extra strength is coming from. Is it in the haunches? The broad flat chest? The arms? Next I look, the table's over. Albert E. is flying through the air. The owner's come out of the kitchen. This is serious business. By this time the place has quieted down. All attention is on the boxers. What's the big guy pissed about? Who's the little fellow?

I edge toward the door, the cause of it all making the grand escape. But Albert E. is not my responsibility, I say in my own defense, to no one in particular. If I went up to stop them, I'd likely get belted in the cross fire. Soon I see six guys holding Albert E., six holding Petronius, their arms pinned back like wings, the cautionary words rising like a hiss, going out in layers across the room. This is some kind of a ritual which men understood better than I do.

Half smile, as the two men pass each other at the end. Hands out timidly. To shake? To beat up on each other again? It isn't exactly clear. Albert E. comes out into the freezing air, dusting off his hands. "I needed some exercise," he says, the blue veins visible under the skin of his fingers, the knuckles starting to swell up. "No, nothing wrong," he says, quietly walking along beside me.

*Meanwhile, Niels Bohr is taking notes again, jotting stuff down in his little leather notebook. When an atom is excited, he begins, to the Mth energy state Em, it can return to some lower energy state in the form of a light quantum. Thus, he concludes, glancing happily at Albert E. and me, we can write:* $HVm.n = Em\text{-}En$ *or* $Vm,n = \dfrac{Em\text{-}En}{h}$.

## The Messenger

Sometimes I believe they are sent to me. God's messengers. To test me. This one never smiled. He stood in the doorway of my office, solid as a tree trunk. The confusion of phones ringing, conversations of colleagues, urgent students, never fazed him. He was his grandmother's emissary.

Which century had he come from? His dark hair was painted onto his head like the Golem's. He stared at me as though I should recognize him. "You wrote the story about Singer," he announced. And then he told me his name. Surely I had never met him before. In fact, I had never seen anyone who looked like him. Thick glasses. Inside them, his eyes floated like carp. I didn't know which one to focus on.

He was clutching a thick manilla envelope, the kind with a red string wound several times around the circular clasp. I offered him a chair. "My grandmother..." he began. I knew before he finished the

sentence. I was to be the literary agent for his grandmother who had spent seven years writing this story.
Well, actually it was a novel. The package contained
a summary and outline of the chapters and a letter
from his grandmother as well as a few sample chapters. I was to find a publisher for his grandmother,
arrange the best deal.

His short thick arms kept making gestures like speech
that can't quite leave the throat of its speaker, quick
jabs. Arms, moving toward me and away, with that
manuscript. I made no move to relieve him of his
burden. I remembered a story about Alexander Pope
who kept his arms folded behind his back on such
occasions so that he would not appear to invite the
flock of pages. But a grandmother. And this boy. An
emissary in the long family of emissaries. She had
written a novel which started with the Bible and span-
ned three millenia. And here was I, the sacred recipient, with my hands tightly clenched behind my back.

My officemate interrupted her conversation with a
student to slyly watch me. But she never said a word
to me about it afterward. I knew she wondered how
I would handle this one. There had been others. Many
others over the years.

The grandmother's novel started in Biblical times,
traveled through the Babylonian exile to the Roman
period, continued to the crusades, took in dozens of
massacres, pogroms, mass suicides, heroic acts, false
messiahs, cabalistic rituals, lingered for quite a time
at the Holocaust and then spread out among the valleys and hills of Israel where it seemed to fuse with
the landscape. Somehow it managed to separate itself
once again, until it rapped soundly upon the door of

the last quarter of the 20th century. It was all there, he assured me, in the package he still tried to shove toward me.

By now, my office chair had rolled into the filing cabinet. Soon I would be near the window. I watched a pigeon making his escape from a window across the parking lot. He was clumsy in his hideous red galoshes. I envied him. I would have done anything at that moment to escape the scrutiny of my messenger. He was so serious, so earnest. He never smiled. He seemed to be taking a reading of my face, each eye deciding for itself. But whatever conclusion he came to, I could not fathom it.

Once, after I had given a talk in a synagogue an old Russian woman named Karamazov invited me to come home with her to live. But first she poured me a cup of tea, fed me three or four cakes, insisted that no one speak to me until I had eaten. She too was a messenger. I knew I must be careful, make no mistake. These messengers were like the Thirty-Six Just, the hearts of the world multiplied, who take upon themselves the suffering of all. It is said that when an unknown Just rises to heaven, God must warm him for a thousand years in his fingers, so frozen is he by the sorrows of this world. Without them, none of the rest of us would be alive.

But I said no to Mrs. Karamazov. I said goodbye to Mrs. Karamazov. And I never understood why I said no. I could feel the messenger recede, my opportunity disappear. I had failed a test whose purpose no one had ever bothered to explain to me.

What could he be thinking? Had he sprung whole cloth from an egg? From the hatchery or the sea? Who was he? Who had sent him to me that afternoon? He had only hesitated briefly at my door. He seemed to know me instinctively, seeking out my face as he pronounced my name. I felt outnumbered by him though I was taller, older. He seemed immovable, like a boulder, like a fire hydrant. He hadn't called to make an appointment. Yet he'd found me in.

"I haven't an agent myself," I heard myself telling him. "I haven't even a publisher," I said plaintively, hoping he'd pity me. "And I don't know anything about novels," I said firmly. This time my chair had wedged itself against the radiator. I felt like I was on fire.

An inspiration: I began pulling open the drawer of the metal filing cabinet. I'd give him a list of agents. I'd find him the name of an editor who had published my article. Let someone else deal with his grand-mother. I'd suffer whatever punishment clearly was in store for me. He didn't move a muscle. He didn't flinch. He didn't change his expression. I watched him as I flurried through the papers in the file cabinet. I opened drawer after drawer, one yellow folder, one green. No luck. Finally I came to the brown paper with an address on it. "Here," I said. "Copy down this address. Give it to your grandmother. No, on second thought, give the whole pamphlet to her. Let her keep it." And I spelled out the name of the editor.

He watched me, somehow unconvinced. He was on another track. Nothing I could do would derail him. "My grandmother," he continued as though his sentence had calmly started years ago, "would like it if you could read her novel and write her a note afterward telling her what you think of it. It would be very important to her."

"January," I muttered, "nothing to read until January," I stuttered, the words coming out wrong, as though January were a soggy log floating in the sea which I had just grabbed ahold of rather than permit myself to drown. "This is the end of the semester," I heard myself tell him. "See these papers?" I threw them up into the air, a whole set of student papers to convince him. He never batted an eyelash. "I have to read all of this first. Besides, I haven't anything to say to a novelist. It wouldn't be of any special use to your grandmother, what I might think of her book."

He rose, he rose in his chair like a battalion of sturdy soldiers, they all ascended with him. The packet still in his hand, he turned away from me and walked slowly, slowly to the door and he never looked back. The place where he had been, that place above the threshold, seemed to retain his shape for a long time afterward.

He is gone now. I do not see him clearly in my mind's eye. But that packet in his hand, those pages which I never asked him to hand to me, the story whose beginning I shall never see—how it burns there in my mind, how it stares at me. How curious I have grown to see how it all began, the letters moving together to make words, the words settling down alongside one another into sentences, the sentences telling their story. For days I have tried to imagine what that old woman could have written, what that solemn boy held in his hands that day. Messenger, emissary, shape in my doorway: Tell me what it was she wrote.

## Albino

When my father died, my mother was unleashed upon the world. The dangerous wistfulness which in a moment could turn to fury broke loose when my father took his hand away from the cover of the box. He had guarded it well enough for years now. But when the blood coursing through sixty-thousand miles of arteries and veins found a small opening in the interior wall of his aorta and forced its way through the ballooning elastic wall of the vessel, he was required to turn his attention to it, all the attention he could muster at the time.

For it was his death he must direct himself to at that moment, his death which greeted him with both arms, causing him to lift ever so slightly his own right arm from the box where what remained of her lay in the tiny white bones assembled to form her name.

And she rose up. I tell you, she rose up with all her

force, like the swirling currents of a tornado, like the atoms of a molecule in their random dance. And she was unleashed upon the world.

He tried to close the lid but the blood which was now escaping through the artery was beginning to make its appearance in his skin, beginning to seep out around the corners of his mouth.

To all appearances things were as they should be. The rescue squad had been called and had arrived. And he, gone upstairs to dress, had gotten as far as removing his robe and pajamas and slippers. Had he a presentiment that his next habitat would be the grave? That he was doing the work for those who might have to? He never liked to trouble others.

So when the rescue squad arrived he was no longer sitting naked in his desk chair but was lying on the floor. The men did not seem concerned with appearances. They felt no need to cover him with a blanket as they worked over him to revive him.

And he, for his part, kept his right hand over the lip of the box for as long as he could. But then his heart stopped. And his breathing. And the byways closed off their trafficking in the globe of his head after a while. And we who were left behind didn't know what happened to him then. He stayed warm for a little. And then he grew cold from the head down. And then he grew stiff. But that took some hours.

And meanwhile the lid opened and my mother rose up in her few bones. She rose up in her robes of light. In her fiery anger she rose up. And he wasn't there to say a word. He wasn't there at all. And she left behind in her box a remnant, one small white knucklebone, dancing on the floor of the wooden box, dancing alone.

At first I did not feel the force of her. I did not feel her anger. When the giant chestnut oak fell across the roof, smashing the asphalt shingles and the wooden frame below, I attributed it to natural causes, the high winds that day, the age of the tree. But the little knucklebone danced merrily on the bottom of its wooden box. It sang a wistful tune. And it left its imprint on the tar paper of the roof, a signature, two indentations and two curved lines.

And when the rain poured in through the eaves, wetting down the pages of her letters, those grim admonitions from all the years, still I said nothing of it, still I did not attribute any of it to her. After all, rain is only rain, that gathering up from the oceans and rivers, that lifting like a skin from the surface of water, up through the air, into clouds and down to us again, only slightly altered in the process.

But when I looked down at my waist this morning and found growing there a forest of mushrooms, the universal veils of each only recently torn, the tiny pigmented remnants of the deadly veil in place on the caps, tawny and poisonous, I knew it was her handiwork. There could be no denying it. And I, who was consigned forever to remain out of the way of the light of the natural world, that world which brought me the only love I have ever known, was to be the harbor and haven for those mysterious growths which prefer darkness and moisture.

I, deprived forever of the coloration native to everything in this world, was to harbor for the rest of my
life the exotic coloration of these growths. I was to
contain in my body and upon its surfaces the life
cycles of any number of these creatures, the four
hundred year silences while the mycelium thickened
within my body, the network establishing itself with
great permanence and invisibility, until the fruiting
bodies appeared, the climate exactly right for their
births upon my skin.

And so I go on, shielding myself from the light, sleeping late until the force of the sun is diminished, and
walking out in the first sign of evening, carrying with
me the moist growths, the stalks and caps multiplying
in my body. Under the white snow clouds of winter
I am at home at last.

# Where We Are Led

When we stood in the schoolyard that day, we covered Our Lady of the Woods, we scrolled it up out of sight and attended only to the bank of trees flowing away from us along the watery air, our feet on the asphalt hopscotch squares. We walked in the schoolyard as though we had all stepped out of a Victorian painting: a few pairs, a small group, the spaces between us suggesting an endless time. Alongside us a girl recited her catechism and the old dog built of peculiarly re-constructed parts lay in the tall grass, his rheumy eyes reflecting the trees. It was bluegreen that day. No one brought a camera. Someone said: Do you see the school house. In the thin rain. Someone answered: I pretend it is not there. Only the trees floating away from us across the watery air. And we started again, leaving the house that day, the front door unlocked, as though at any moment we would return. We walked out toward the street and bent low under the branches, bark beneath our feet, the damp cold of

December, until we came to a clearing, a field and the schoolyard. In a little it would be totally dark. It was too warm to snow. The nuns came out of Our Lady of the Woods and knelt down in the field, holding their rosaries against their bodies as if they might take wing. Everywhere we looked there were dark and light nuns, the field was covered with them. Though their mouths moved in prayer, we heard only the sounds their broad sleeves made as they lifted and lowered their arms.

# Whose Hands Are These?

I am lying under Baby's blanket. My feet stick out.
A mauve cloud has gathered overhead, the tension
gone slack on the rope between us. Baby doesn't know
we wear it, the rope.

Under the blanket I can still smell her. I imagine how
my hands feel around her waist, the way she shudders
as I bring her toward me, hold her close, the pink
wooly garment she wears turning her into something
atavistic.

I remember her in the mornings, how the cool air
blows at her new hair. The way her teeth look, the
ones that erupted in her upper gums only this morning, the canines. Perfectly matched and on opposing
sides. On the bottom there are two white ridged in-
cisors all the way out, like sharp blossoms.

When I feed Baby, she holds up one hand; the other

is tucked behind me, walking along my side, squeez-
ing and pinching, feeling the soft material of my
blouse as though it were the time long ago when her
mother suckled her.

Now she holds up her free hand, floats it like a sea
anemone over her head watching the fingers open and
close.

One night she reached into the mirror with her right
hand, only to be stopped at the hard surface. Then
she drew the hand back and approached its image
again, the fingers moving sinuously toward and away.
She drew her mouth to the glass and kissed the other
baby. She lingered there. Then she cried a bit. Such
a hard baby. So unyielding. She watched the child
carefully, her eyes darkening. Then she cried once
hard, sighed deeply and asked to be lifted up into my
arms again.

What does she know? we ask her. Which of us does
she recognize? Whose hands are those? Do they belong
to her body?

One morning the sky opened unexpectedly and its
pillow of white feathers began to spill from the sky.
Baby was talking to the baby on the jar of beans she
was eating when she caught sight of the first white
feather. Take me out, she shouted, rocking back and
forth. I unbuckled the several restraints, lifted the tray
from her chair, and swooped her up into my arms.
She nuzzled briefly, leaving a trail of sticky green
across my chest and shoulder. Then she smiled and
the sun filled these rooms.

Out, out, she demanded, her body struggling toward the kitchen door. I raced toward the kitchen, lifted the chain lock, released the dead bolt, turned the key, the knob and we descended into the morning air. All around us the curved white feathers floated and fell to the ground. On the ground they reassembled, becoming ducks, swans and chickens. There was a terrible crowing, hissing and quacking. But Baby didn't seem to mind at all. Over there, she kept pointing and shouted while I raced about through the backyard, so she could touch first one, then another feather. I stooped low as I fled through the yard so she could feel the neck of a chicken, a duck, a swan. The hissing of the swans didn't alarm her. She grew more eager. Beneath me, the ground grew slippery with the layers of feathers.

Each day a new season presented itself for Baby's benefit. Summer arrived on Saturday. The birds took up their positions in the trees and along the telephone wires. A red-headed woodpecker got started again on the holes he had begun the summer before along the eastern border of the house. When Baby came back into the house she craned upwards all day looking at the white ceiling as though it could give way to sky, as though at any moment a leafy crown of tree would suddenly emerge through the ceiling bearing its usual portion of birds.

On Sunday the leaves fell down. Baby sat on the cold stoop eating crisp brown poplar leaves. Some were indented with sharp points. Baby shouted as the points stung her tender cheeks. Her four sharp teeth worked at the leaves, melting them into a kind of algae. The saliva she secreted acted like the enzymes mushrooms make to break down and devour wood. Nothing was safe from Baby.

On Monday Baby ate the tax returns. She carefully tore apart the pages, having first unwedged them from their low shelf in the bookcase. Then she held them in place with her foot while she went at them with her fingers. Those delicate blossoms tore into the tax forms as though they were the FBI. She tested first for flavor and then ripped off one corner, then the next, eating as she went along. At times she would glance over the figures as though she could read them, to check the addition. You've made a mistake here, she would shout. You owe the government another four hundred dollars, she would say, swallowing the column.

Baby wearied of this meal. Night, shouted Baby and the stars appeared in the sky. Night, she shrieked and the moon lifted away from her hand and floated up, clicking into place. Night, she said again, and it was fully dark then.

Day, she taunted. The sun bobbled over obliterating the moon. The darkness fell away. Day, shouted Baby. The morning winds came up, the birds lifted their wings shyly from their faces and started to sing. The waterfalls sent their waters cascading over the rocks, the flowers lifted their weary petals and opened all at once. Day, said Baby contentedly, and closed her eyes. It was time for Baby's morning nap.

Stretch out, I instructed Baby. She planted herself like a wedge in her baby carriage, her feet pressed against the foot of the carriage, her head at the top, smiling warily. We're leaving, I announced, wheeling her through the rooms like a newborn. Faster, she screamed. I rushed through the rooms, the books on the shelves, the records going by in a blur. Faster. To the kitchen, she commanded. I rushed around the curve in the hall. The carriage stuck between the doorway molding and the wall. Idiot, Baby shouted. Milk, Baby demanded, reclining, her head on the yellow polkadot pillow, her toes pointing skyward, her finger wagging at me while the other hand drifted dreamily above her in its sea anemone position.

Sometimes Baby tugs at the rope but I pretend not to notice. She grows angry, her face reddens. She tugs again. What is it, Baby? I ask innocently. I slacken the tension on the rope. Baby picks cheerios out of the couch. Or searches for a cat's whisker. Or arches her back as though to begin an enormous tantrum but she forgets halfway through what it was about. Sometimes the finches fly through these rooms calling to Baby but she is busy searching for her toes.

One day a little groove started to etch its way into Baby's gray matter. Hi, Baby said to no one in particular. Hi, she said again. The groove deepened. A small channel formed. Hi, Baby said it all afternoon. Then it disappeared forever. Say Hi, we said to Baby. Hi, Hi. Hi, we said smiling and waving to Baby. She looked dumbly out at us. You started it, we told Baby. Say Hi, Baby. She looked sweetly at us and gave the Bronx cheer.

Once the rope stretched from my house to Baby's. But now I am no longer safe in my own house. I float out into the world, going wherever Baby chooses to go, tethered by her rope. I have become airy, my hands like sea anemone. I bring them before my face. I ask: Whose hands are these?

# Saturday Afternoon At The Movies

Now this will be something to talk about—how she
sat on his lap during the Saturday matinee and they
rocked quietly together through the Western until the
guns went off and the horses started to gallop and
their soft moans and the wet that was beginning to
go between them all came to a head at the same moment so no one could tell for sure if it was the gunshot
or the hooves of the horses or the advancing Indians
or the two of them letting the sounds go between
their teeth while their eyes never once wavered from
the screen.

# A Little Sex Goes A Long Way

He hummed it to himself as he drove along. A little sex goes a long way. A little sex . . . a little sex . . . goes a long . . . waaaaaay.

I'm wearing my raincoat, she had whispered into the receiver in her husky voice at two in the morning. And there's nothing on under it.

I'll be right over, he said. He hopped out of bed and glided along the street to his car, his feet barely touching the ground. The distance between his place and hers disappeared like a stretch of ocean you maneuver without realizing you're making any headway at all. He was daydreaming as he chugged toward her. This time he was somewhere in North Africa.

*Omar stayed a precise six feet behind Yacout in the medina. Every so often as she turned her dark head toward him he opened his hand to reveal the stolen watches partially concealed in a soiled handerchief. Beside him wandered a young beggar woman carrying an infant. Dirhams, she pleaded, tapping him lightly on the arm. Dirhams, she grew more insistent. Yacout strayed into the outer fringes of a circle of people gathered around a snake charmer and his cobra. His blue eyes were clouded by cataracts. Sensing her presence there, he turned his body stiffly toward her as though he were realigning himself along the earth's axis. The tight circle opened, making room for her. She looked down at the head of the snake poised in the air beneath her, its tongue streaming out into the space between them. Above her head a great serpent hung down supported by enormous baskets of living seed, these suspended from the live hands of the universe, the fingers of the enchanter. The creature stiffened as it moved, twisting and turning as it bore down, as it penetrated, the narrow fork of its tongue arching out. The limbless one moved like the waters of a moving river, each motion recorded deep within her body.*

The light turned red just before he got to the intersection. He stepped on the brake automatically. The donut shop was still open. He could see the girl inside at the counter pouring herself some hot coffee, licking the sugary crumbs from the corner of the metal tray.

*She is putting him into her mouth, holding him lightly between her lips, keeping her teeth back and apart, the way the bitch holds onto her pups. And he gets big while her tongue circles him. He has his hands on her breasts, making her nipples stand up hard, tasting her and she is moving and making sounds and he goes quiet and she knows he is liking it and that nobody's ever done it this way to him before. She knows by the way he lets his legs go apart.*

He shifts from neutral to first, pushing down the clutch pedal and letting it up slowly, feeling the first point of resistance as he gives her some gas and moves through the intersection. There isn't much traffic at this hour. He leans back against the seat, breathes deeply and looks out in front of him again.

*Well, what have you done today at work, she is asking him as he comes through the front door. He removes his left shoe, his green sock and holds his foot out to her. She takes it in her hand, drawing the leg nearer, reading on the sole of his left foot the carefully prepared message: Yea though I walk through the valley of the shadow of death I shall fear no evil. On the right, which he has just unveiled, there is another message. She cannot decipher it. She holds a mirror to his foot, thinking it is some kind of trick, but it does not help. And you, he asks her, what have you written today. She pulls her skirt up above her knees and shows him the short poem inscribed on her thigh. Well done, he says admiringly. A good day's work, he tells her, moving his lips over each letter and word.*

He leans forward to stare out at the road. Something is lying in the street. He hopes it won't cause him any delay.

*He is kneeling on the floor beneath her, her blue velvet shirt covering her hips, the red hairs curling out near his mouth. While she moves from place to place he brings his tongue near her, sometimes touching her with the tip, sometimes tasting only the air between them.*

Once he had sucked too hard on a glass pipette and had drawn up a few extra cc's of E. Coli which made him sick for days. She told him she had once swallowed some riboflavin she was pipetting. The stench of it and the texture were nauseating but instead of making her ill, her long red hair was brighter than usual, her fair skin unblemished, and she seemed to thrive. He thought about the scar on her abdomen. He liked to run his fingers along the raised white line, liked to imagine the exotic flower shapes growing unbidden inside her. He wanted to be able to see that mysterious cave where her children would take root and form. He had one more turn to make, a steep right up the hill and he'd be there. The distance between them expanded and contracted at will.

*On a spring day in April they are sitting by a creek, the light forming a ring of color about each thing it touched. He looked at her face, her hair caught in that light. Her lips brushed his arm. And the light bound them together, painted them into that scene. The mystery of that moment often came back to him like the day he had drawn her initials into the sand next to his own.*

He wasn't sure how he'd gotten to her door or beyond it into her arms. But he was there all right. He could tell by the heavy breathing, the odor of sex. He stretched himself out on her bed, breathed deeply like a man about to go under water and set into her. Say it, he urged her. He always wanted her to say it. She liked teasing him, making him wait, holding out. He liked that too, prolonging things. Say it now, he urged again.

Please fuck me, she whispered to his elbow. Somehow they never quite lined up. Please fuck me, she said. This time he already was. She said it again, insistently.

Say it, he whispered. Say it again. The short rhythms of his ejaculation were building, setting off layers of waves deep inside her, starting up elongated waves that moved in slow motion and seemed to rise up through her body. They were both coming at once and he was urging her: Say it, say it again. And she was calling, calling softly to him across a great distance. Fuck me, please fuck me. And he was. He already was.

# Getting There

Aaron and Joseph, as the sisters were called—their mother had taken quite literally the injunction to name after the dead—struggled to find the route to the cemetery. One drove, the other navigated. When they were sufficiently lost, they reversed roles.

There was a ritual uncertainty about getting to the cemetery. Charts and maps were prepared beforehand. Bridges were accounted for; alternate routes studied and rehearsed. But even as they drove, the road stretched out before them, increasing itself to the horizon; their small green car appeared to be making no headway at all. Joseph would cheerfully call out the route names and landmarks, sanctifying each with her voice, enveloping them as if she were wrapping Chinese pastries.

But nothing helped. How many times they had come to bury members of their family. To unveil headstones. To plant on the graves. The sisters would drive bravely through the day, plotting their course, adjusting the route to account for the mysterious streets which flung themselves helter skelter like barricades along their passage.

The first tombstones rose up like living matter, fitful and silent in the distance. What they had been avoiding during the long drive loomed before them now. But what was it? The fact of the bones floating in the wooden boxes, the flesh seeping away through two holes in the bottom of the coffin? Or the hands of the Kohanim carved into the tombstones, the paired fingers pointing stiffly like the horns of a ram, making the priestly benediction? All those hands, loosened from their owners, more accusation than blessing? Or the souls who wandered ceaselessly in the graveyard, stripped of their husks of speech? No word to divert them. Their space in the world unoccupied.

Or was it the thought of their own deaths they had wished to avoid? The territory between themselves and these souls seemed discontinuous, a place they couldn't negotiate. The two sisters had come this far. But the rest of the journey?

Like the dividing line which separated portions of time. Like that instant when the millenium would turn and nineteen hundred and ninety-nine years would simply fall back into the sleep of years.

Some equated this event with total annihilation. Others saw nothing spectacular about it. Some skipped over the present and rushed headlong into the future. Others lagged behind. And some hid under a bush.

But the two sisters, Joseph and Aaron, were looking backward together. Which gave them both the illusion of looking head, of reading things to come. Aaron had wondered when her mother left them one cold February morning where she was going next. She had carried her mother in her small basket of skin up to the edge of the welcoming glass, but who, she had asked, would pour her like wine to its vessel? Who would take her the rest of the way? How would the heritage go on?

Ø

With her heel braced against the lip of the sharp metal shovel, Aaron set her weight against the earth, pitching this way and that until a clump of clay and grass gave way. Those who had come to pray were disturbed by the work of the sisters. Several, interrupting their prayers, went to the caretaker's house to report them. The pious swayed and bent their knees. They prayed above the dead like dark angels. Their cadillacs shone patent leather black in the September sun. The attack dogs strained on their leashes and the alarm system sent up a wall of sound even Joshua couldn't have brought down. The sisters transported green hoses, turned on faucets, measured out root hormone, fertilizer and moist humus. They dug into the graves as if they meant to disinter their parents.

Ø

The prayers of the pious rose up into the trees, opening and closing their wings as if they planned to roost there for all of eternity. There was about this season a heightened urgency to mend one's fences, to repent, to visit the neglected dead. The small pebbles left by

the visitors on the graves pulled themselves into letters. Some spelled out secret messages from the living.
Others carried the sleeping words of those buried
beneath the stones—warnings and forecasts. Com-
plaints.

There were more arguments in this season than usual.
And more reconciliations. The prayers twittered in
the trees, giving off those last chattering songs before
they grew silent.

∅

The sisters took pains not to disturb Crankshaw's
grave. Some Crankshaw descendant was bound to
turn up, to become indignant at the sight of tan bark
and humus sliding down toward Crankshaw's space,
even if the magnolia tree would someday provide
shade for all of them. Perhaps a succulent blossom
would fall upon Crankshaw's portion, close enough
to his grave for him to inhale the lemon odor and
remember the world.

They were kneeling in the ditch they had created
above their parents, the humus floating like an enormous black planet in the pool of water where it had
not yet been mixed with soil, when they caught sight
of two brown shoes. Joseph tilted her head upward,
taking in a pair of checkered trousers, a flannel shirt
and, above that, a furious face.

"What do you THINK you're DOINGGG? DO
YOU have a PERmit?" They looked at each other,
their arms sunk to the elbows in the mixture of earth
and water.

"What do we need a permit for?" they said in unison. "You gonna git me in trouble," Afikomen said, wagging his finger at the sisters. "You know it!" In the distance the collard greens and radish plants spread luxuriously across the grass. "I'd like to be buried over there," Aaron told him, trying to get him off the subject of permits. "You must have a thing for swamp rats," he nodded toward his garden laughing. "Over the fence then," she said. "Outside this place."

He laughed again. "You pining for St. E's?" he wanted to know. "Can't wait to git back?" Their two laughters twined about each other like the two wicks of the bridal candle, rose up into the trees and settled alongside the prayers.

"You still need a permit," he said. "For what?" Aaron asked him. "For putting in that tree. Don't want no trees overshadowing the tombstones. Some Crankshaw relative fit to be tied. Can't show no partiality here," Afikomen went on.

"Oh that," Aaron said. "That's no tree, only a little bush. Won't amount to anything," she said, bending protectively over its four-foot rise, causing its branches, already budding, to fold over themselves, to shorten.

Ø

Whenever it got too crowded in the cemetery or the trees bent under the weight of the prayers, Afikomen would roll back a year. Slowly, slowly, one would fall away. Nineteen hundred years took a long time to get rid of. The hole in the cemetery filled up with them; they crowded upon one another until they spilled over the top of the hole and spread out along a hillside. Afikomen turned the crank until more of the years fell back. They swelled up in the conservative graveyard where the living wore prayer shawls and covered their heads and only prayed in Hebrew. The years fled through the wire gauge fence into the re-form graveyard where everyone spoke in English and where the dead sat up from time to time to see what was happening. "We can't have this," the orthodox rabbi shouted, seeing the years coming toward him from the two cemeteries.

∅

"What about them?" Joseph demanded of Afikomen, pointing to the recently deceased, resting in their holes, the plastic green carpets covering the true grass and earth surrounding them. "What do they have to say about all of this?" she said, looking up the hill to the place where the long dead resided, where the in-fants had been buried, their tiny headstones long since hidden within the gutted trunks of old trees.

"Oh them, they don't bother me none," he told her. "On a day when I don't feel like working, they tell me not to bother. We gets on just fine. On a day when I'm in the mood to work, they tell me 'That's good.' I keep track of the babies," he said, more to himself than to her.

∅

On the road home Aaron and Joseph passed a dead squirrel. "That little squirrelly spirit is in God's hand now," Joseph said softly. "What did you say?" Aaron asked her.

"God isn't in heaven," Joseph ventured carefully. "I don't know where he is. And the squirrel isn't there on the road either; there's nothing left of him. By tomorrow we won't see any of him. But the squirrelly part, that's what God puts into his hand."

Closer to home, Aaron took her sister to see the leaves. Aaron parked the car and walked out to touch one. She held its huge green face in her arms, running her fingers along its smooth, rubbery surface. Up ahead, there was a year neither of them was likely to get to, a year when the centuries would fall back into the sleep of centuries, when the millennium would turn. Some would cross over that edge; some would walk across that line into a new place. Others would never be able to look over it, the way Moses could not get a good view of Canaan, the way he could not walk into the place with his own feet. But that line was all they could think of now. It drew them toward itself, drew them forward like a huge magnet, iron filings like minutes, like years spilling toward the future.

There

Under the dead surface, you surge toward me and then draw back. What realm supports you now and what necessity leaves me struggling after you here on the surface, parted by this membranous divide? I enfold you, what of you chooses to come this close. By this method you enter my body and are lost in me.

For is it not so that I fall asleep with my hands on my own body. Or that my words going out can find no suitable place for landing. And when I stand in the company of others, when I have gathered my clothing about me and risen to say good night I am surprised by the weight of the cold which I draw about my own shoulders.

Or when you withdrew from me in a day not so different from this one, your skull seemed to shrink between my two hands. This is the world. This is the world with its circuitry ranging between there and here like an animal grazing.

In the season of your death I cannot enter the room for the saying of a thing without encountering the danger of fusion. Past and future support me on either side like two crutches while in the doorway the shadow of my life goes on ahead testing the unknown ground.

# Valentine's Day

The side of her face showed bone. My sister wheeled her into the living room. I stood to the right, watching her. For more than a day she had not been able to eat or drink. My sister sewed bright red cloth napkins. She appliqued red hearts on the tablecloth. There was a cake. One of the children brought candles. It wasn't anyone's birthday. My sister thought it would be a good idea. I wasn't sure. Propping up the dead, I said to myself. Ashamed to have thought it.

*July the eighth: Today she gave me a ruler which curls up like a roll of postage stamps. Last week she offered me her blankets. I refused. The week before—sheets. I took them. Before that, Father's pajamas. Her nightgown. I dream I am in the Convent of the Dominican Sisters where she is playing the piano. It is cool and dark.*

The green tank arrived this morning. The plastic hose and nose pieces. My sister taught us how to set the gauge. She was matter-of-fact. I forgot to be afraid.

My sister stood near her bed. She watched as the oxygen hissed and then hummed through the tubing. As it went into her nostrils.

*July the thirteenth: She dreamed that mice have entered the bed where she is sleeping. Father is waving a broom handle to chase them away but he is unable to rid her bed of them. She has gathered up the mice which the child let loose in the pump-house and set them down again in her dream. Meanwhile inside the main house the mice continue to breed. And in her body the cells of the tumors divide and increase. And her dreams increase. And her dreamless nights are counted and stored and divided among the children.*

Her hair is falling out again. My sister combed it with a silver comb. She pinned up what was left with hair-pins. Then she washed her face. We took turns looking through the buttons in her sewing basket. A green felt button from her coat during the Second World War. Black Persian lamb button. Plastic buckle for a cloth belt. Light green velvet from a dress made of her dead sister's cape. Shirred front. We took turns wearing it.

*July the twentieth: She has grown thin. Through the lenses of her glasses I come across her eyes. I try to bring her back to me. From the great distance where she is traveling. In her dream a telephone is ringing. She goes to it, picks up the receiver. Her dead sister is on the line.*

This morning my sister arrived in time to help her as she vomited. Then my sister emptied the curved stainless steel basin and washed out the blood and vomit from the bedclothes. If it bothered her, she did not let me see. In the evening Father slept in her room. He got up each hour to tend to her.

*September the fifth: I have begun to hold my breath. As in the child's game—statues. To stop. Wherever you are. Your arms still in the position of motion. The echo of each movement in your fingers. She has decided to live until spring. She goes out to the porch at evening to bring the flowers that Father has grown for her. Marigolds the color of light which is withdrawing. As though someone were pulling at a veil of light, uncovering each tree and house which beneath the veil is completely dark.*

She asked for a section of orange. My sister peeled away the thick skin, divided the sections and put one in her mouth. The next morning my sister found it lying inside her cheek.

*A Friday in October: On the page where I have been drawing I see I have made a knife.*

A neighbor came up from downstairs. Everyone was seated around the maple dining room table. My sister wheeled her up close. There were bright favors, candy hearts and a birthday cake with no candles. She smiled. She was no longer able to talk.

*November 25: She dreamed that Father was driving the car. Next to him in the front seat was a dead man talking continuously.*

My sister poured the tea, cut the cake. We sang to her. She sat straight up in her wheel chair. She could not drink the tea.

*December 26: When she was born, no one believed she would live. They brought her home to die. Her sister sang to her and they sewed small white gloves to cover her hands so she would not scratch herself. Each one took a turn watching over her.*

My sister said: The condemned ate a hearty breakfast on the eighth day. The doctor told us she would die today. My sister must have believed she would live. How else could she have made such a huge cauldron of soup.

*December 27: She thinks of a line of poetry. Looking out between the slats of the blinds in her bedroom she says:*

> *the white*
> *the overhanging*
> *cloud*

*My sister dipped four Q-tips into grape juice so she could suck the liquid from the cotton.*

*February 10: Her head between my two hands has grown small.*

I did not do my part. That is why I cannot remember these events clearly. When someone was needed to bring oxygen, place the plastic tubes in her nostrils, I managed not to be in the room. Or when she had soiled the bed, I called for my sister. The day a slice of orange lay like a curved moon inside her cheek, it was not I who put fingers into her mouth to remove it. Nor was I there to hear her say how the disease had used her up. The others have wanted to write a proper account of all this. I have not encouraged them.

# Mushroom

Ø

Each has its moment for standing erect on the earth.
Is it not so that we come to ripeness. All is directed
toward it. No matter that we struggle against the
river. That we dig in with our heels and call out our
various refusals.

These fungi, swimming in the earth, amniotic sacs
tied about them like wings, have burst forth with
such pressure they bring patches of moss up on their
outspread tablets, shedding the flexible skin along
their stalks like a woman's slip bunched at her ankles.

Ø

All for one purpose. Only this. To open the edges of
the canopy. To spread apart the thin ridges, gills. To
release the spore, billions going out into sunlight. We
read in them the whole stubborn history. They scatter,

taking root in their kingdom of randomness. And the pileus, tawny cap, gathers moisture to its center like a glistening crown.

And goes down. If at night the fruiting body edges to black and doesn't regain itself and leaves us no visible message but huddles in the depths of some primordial silence until the moment is right again for another arrival, filaments riding the substratum, pairing and separating and fusing again in the sacred ritual underground, we will wait.

Sometimes we wanted them to be missing. The cycle so swift it took place while we were sleeping. Or its final stages closed down in the first hours of morning so we were given the black remnants, spores long since scattered. Or when we went to look—only the outline, like fingerprints, the indelible signature of a vanished tribe.

Or we wanted to intervene. To tear the cap from its stalk and examine the white ridges or the gnarled surface coated with warts, to touch the gray flesh until our own mark on it turned it blue. To force the orange-red milk through the broken skin.

But they live in their own life. The vaulting upward. Opening a way through the network of moss, making the first undulating appearance, gelatinous drop in the narrow opening. This blind tunneling to delicate petals and wings. Male and female in one site.

You knelt down and drank from the well carved out in the center of the pileus. The fresh water from recent rain tasted of ozone, lightning still in it. The red up-ward thrusting pileus moved in you. Earth containing the male element. Air, the opening female. Mysteri-ous reversals, both entering and entered.

With infinite patience you waited to grow still enough, to become small until you could move easily under them like an insect. Shield, housetop, umbrella, canopy of flesh hovering steadily over you. You waited until the objects of the earth backed off. Only this, spores reticulated like shining crystals, falling in a rain about you.

And you lay down with the weight of them above you like snow and the rhythm of your own flesh stilled like fire which is subdued by water. And now the strains of a small music came to you. The rubbing of the fruiting body as it passed out of the matrix of the mycelium beneath, as it thrust forth through the earth. The sudden unfastening of the integument from the stalk. The sound of the canopy opening. Hypae filling with fluid and extending. And the sound of the spores falling.

A drop of milk of the Lactarius gathered on the stem and fell to earth just past your body and spores washed along the lawn in its wake. You could hear the dark spent ones lean into each other, hear them split open or press downward against the stem.

You slept then. Across the low green a shadow grew
lengthwise and filled with weight. The spirits beneath
it recited a verse for the dangerous hour. The eye
following the trail of the mushroom, omitting all
else—like tracking the nucleus of a great comet—for-
saking green leaves, narrow stems, a thousand species
of insect, attending only to this alphabet of fruiting
bodies, eye trained to these structures alone, reading
in the terrible scattering its own solitary nature.

∅

And the spores rose. Suspended more than seven miles
above the surface of the earth. The pendants of rain
were heavily laden with them at first but later they
were missing. Ornaments with spines, ridged or
whiskered, oval, spherical or crescent shaped, spiral
springs to fit this coiled bit of life for its long voyage
to a region alien and rare, its arrival into the future.

Nothing has been said here of subversion—this lan-
guage up on a stem. Nothing of these spores streaming
out over the earth or storing the components of an
epoch in strands like a package set down under a street
lamp, along a window ledge, a word or number to
be gathered up later in some sequence other than its
own, holy strand outlining in its very nature the ingre-
dients of what is to come. Spores so buoyant that a
beam of light passing through a tube in which they
are falling will create air currents strong enough to
send them churning up like smoke from a puffing
locomotive.

∅

Attend to these uprising in the summer solstice, to these small births upon the surface of the earth. Afterward is, after all, only heresay, Lovely but speculative. You must hurry to see this. In an hour the spores will be shed, the strange cap still wearing bits of the universal veil will turn color and later walking there you will think it is only a leaf turned brown until your foot touching it senses its spongy depth.

Remember this birth like a covenant, this coming to ripeness, the small deaths played out again. Take them to yourself. For who is it uses us? Our uprisings and our deaths? For whom is it we bring again the apprenticeship of knowledge? In order that we needn't begin over again.

*Solstice*
*Summer 1981*

# Myra Sklarew

learned to read music before English. Wrote stories
because of teacher in third grade who often went to
the window to cry. The stories seemed to help. First
story was about mushrooms. So with a long piece in
this collection. Studied bacterial genetics and bacterial
viruses at Cold Spring Harbor Biological Institute
under Dr. Salvadore Luria. Earned B. S. in biology
from Tufts. Worked as a pianist in a dance band
playing for Polish, Czech, Italian dance halls and
after-hours taverns. Worked as a cashier in a 5 & 10;
typist in a state mental hospital; bookkeeper in a beer
company; lab tech (chemical assays and cholesterol
studies involving feeding experiments and autopsies);
research assistant, Yale University School of
Medicine, Department of Neurophysiology. Worked
under Karl Pribram studying frontal lobe function of
Rhesus monkeys until imminent birth of girl child
prevented her from catching monkeys in wire cage.
Taught and directed MFA Program in Creative
Writing at The American University, 17 years.
Published six poetry collections. In 1972 awarded di
Castagnola Award from the Poetry Society of
America; National Jewish Book Council Award in
Poetry in 1977.